Diego Saves the Tree Frogs

adapted by Sarah Willson
based on the original teleplay by Madellaine Paxson
illustrated by Susan Hall

SCHOLASTIC INC.

New York Toronto London Auckland Sydney
Mexico City New Delhi Hong Kong Buenos Aires

Hi! I am  .

DIEGO

This is  .

BABY JAGUAR

I hear some  .

TREE FROGS

They need our help!

Hi,  !
ALICIA

 is my sister.
ALICIA

Hurry,  !
ALICIA

Tell us about  .
TREE FROGS

 live

TREE FROGS

in the rainforest.

Some

TREE FROGS

have  eyes.

RED

TREE FROGS have strong . **LEGS**

Their  **LEGS** help them

to jump high.

TREE FROGS have sticky . **TOES**

Their  **TOES** help them

to climb.

is our camera.

CLICK

 found the !

CLICK   TREE FROGS

Do you see the ?

TREE FROGS

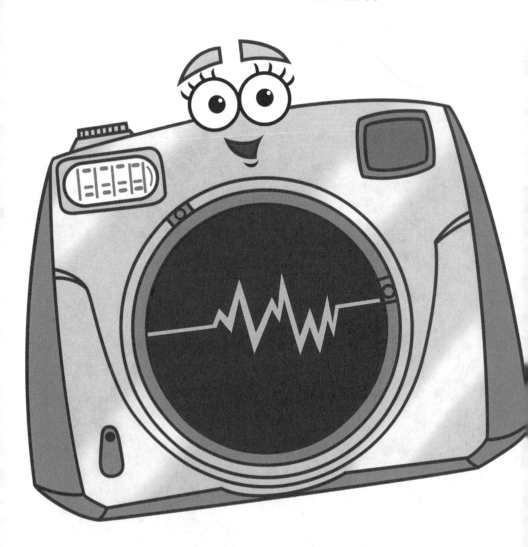

The  fell!
TREE FROGS

They are on a 🌿.
BRANCH

The 🌿 is in the 〰️!
BRANCH   RIVER

Come on. We need to save the  !
TREE FROGS

Look out for the  !
COCONUTS

Jump like a 🐸 .
TREE FROG

Jump over the 🥥 !
COCONUTS

The went

TREE FROGS

into the ▲.

PYRAMID

How will we get inside?

Do you see a ▮?

DOOR

I need my sticky .
GLOVES

My  help me climb
GLOVES

like a .
TREE FROG

We made it!

Do you see the  TREE FROGS ?

Oh, no! The  !
WATERFALL

Tell the TREE FROGS

to jump!

The  jumped.

TREE FROGS

They are safe.

I will take them home.

ALICIA found a new TREE for the TREE FROGS.

The new  is strong.
The new is safe.

TREE

TREE

The  are happy.
TREE FROGS

They love their new .
TREE

We saved the  !

TREE FROGS